The Night Before Christmas

CLEMENT CLARKE MOORE

Illustrated by Heather Brown

Piggy Toes
PRESS

Copyright © 2022 Bendon, Inc. Published by Piggy Toes Press, an imprint of Bendon, Inc.

'Twas the night before Christmas,
when all through the house
Not a creature was stirring,
not even a mouse.

The stockings were hung
by the chimney with care,
In hopes that St. Nicholas
soon would be there.

The children were nestled
all snug in their beds,
While visions of sugarplums
danced in their heads.

And Mamma in her 'kerchief,
    and I in my cap,
Had just settled down
    for a long winter's nap,

When out on the lawn
  there arose such a clatter,
I sprang from the bed
  to see what was the matter.

Away to the window
  I flew like a flash,
Tore open the shutters,
  and threw up the sash.

The moon on the breast
  of the new-fallen snow
Gave the luster of midday
  to objects below,

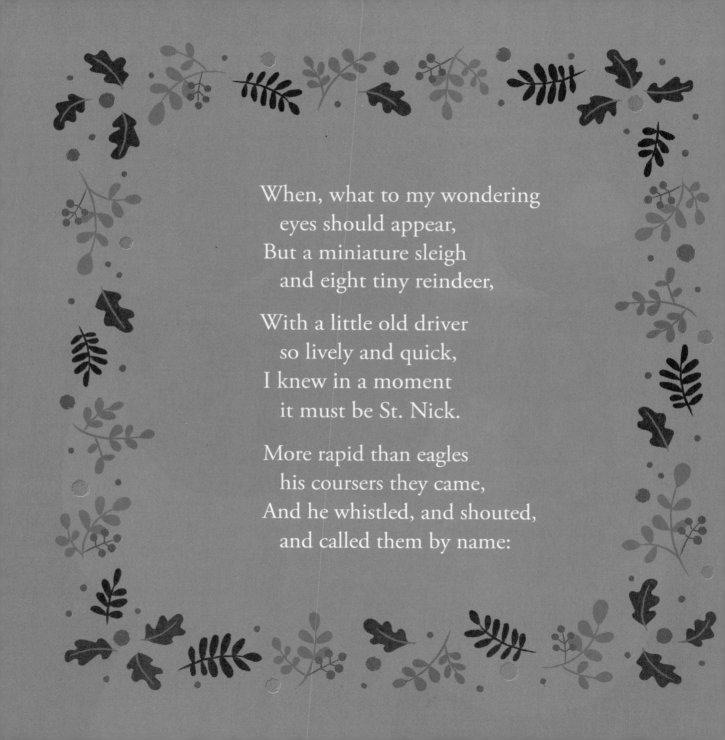

When, what to my wondering
   eyes should appear,
But a miniature sleigh
   and eight tiny reindeer,

With a little old driver
   so lively and quick,
I knew in a moment
   it must be St. Nick.

More rapid than eagles
   his coursers they came,
And he whistled, and shouted,
   and called them by name:

d Vixen!

, Donder and Blitzen!

To the top of the porch!
to the top of the wall!
Now, dash away! dash away!
dash away, all!"

As dry leaves that before
    the wild hurricane fly,
When they meet with an obstacle,
    mount to the sky,

So up to the housetop
    the coursers they flew,
With the sleigh full of toys,
    and St. Nicholas too.

And then, in a twinkling,
    I heard on the roof
The prancing and pawing
    of each little hoof.

As I drew in my head,
and was turning around,
Down the chimney St. Nicholas
came with a bound.

He was dressed all in fur,
    from his head to his foot,
And his clothes were all tarnished
    with ashes and soot.

A bundle of toys
    he had flung on his back,
And he looked like a peddler
    just opening his pack.

His eyes—how they twinkled!
    his dimples—how merry!
His cheeks were like roses,
    his nose like a cherry!

His droll little mouth
    was drawn up like a bow,
And the beard of his chin
    was as white as the snow.

The stump of a pipe
    he held tight in his teeth,
And the smoke it encircled
    his head like a wreath.

He had a broad face
    and a little round belly
That shook when he laughed,
    like a bowlful of jelly.

He was chubby and plump—
    a right jolly old elf;
And I laughed when I saw him,
    in spite of myself.

A wink of his eye
    and a twist of his head
Soon gave me to know
    I had nothing to dread.

He spoke not a word,
     but went straight to his work,
And filled all the stockings—
     then turned with a jerk;

And laying his finger
   aside of his nose,
And giving a nod,
   up the chimney he rose!

He sprang to his sleigh,
    to his team gave a whistle,
And away they all flew
    like the down of a thistle.

But I heard him exclaim,
    ere he drove out of sight:

"Happy Christmas to all,
and to all a good night!"